MARC BROWN

ARTHUR BABYSITS

Little, Brown and Company

Boston   Toronto   London

With love and thanks to some great readers and writers:
Barbara Bush; Ms. Cassell's class in Terre Haute, Indiana;
and Mary Etta Bitter's class in Lakewood, Ohio

Copyright © 1992 by Marc Brown

First Edition

Library of Congress Cataloging-in-Publication Data

Brown, Marc Tolon.
    Arthur babysits : an Arthur adventure / Marc Brown.—1st ed.
      p.   cm.
    Summary: Arthur's experience babysitting for the terrible Tibble
twins is as challenging as he expected, but he finally gets control
by telling them a spooky story.
    ISBN 0-316-11293-3
    [1. Animals—Fiction.   2. Babysitters—Fiction.]   I. Title.
PZ7.B81618A1   1992
[E]—dc20   91-46516

10 9 8 7 6 5 4 3

Published simultaneously in Canada
by Little, Brown & Company (Canada) Limited

Printed in the United States of America

Arthur's sister D.W. had a problem.
"The Tibble twins are visiting again, and they're driving
me crazy!" she said. "They're everywhere I go."
"Oh, they can't be that bad," said Arthur.
"How would you know?" said D.W.

Later that afternoon, Arthur and D.W. took Kate for a walk.
"Look!" shouted the Tibble twins. "There's D.W.!"
"Oh, no!" said D.W. "Quick, let's hide."
Mrs. Tibble looked worried.
"I'm in a terrible pickle," she said. "I need a sitter for my
grandsons tonight, and I can't find one anywhere."
"Arthur can do it!" said D.W. "He babysits me all the time."
"Oh, Arthur, you're a lifesaver!" said Mrs. Tibble. "I'll call
your mother and set it up right now."

"Babysitting is such a big responsibility," said Arthur.
"I'm a little nervous."
"You'll do a fine job," said Mother.
"We'll be right here if you want to call us," said Father.
"Here's my crash helmet," said D.W. "You'll need it!"
"Why?" asked Arthur. "Are you coming along?"
"You think *I'm* trouble?" said D.W. "Just wait."

On the way, Arthur walked by the Sugar Bowl.
"Hey, Arthur," called Buster, "where are you going?"
"I'm on my way to babysit for Mrs. Tibble," said Arthur.

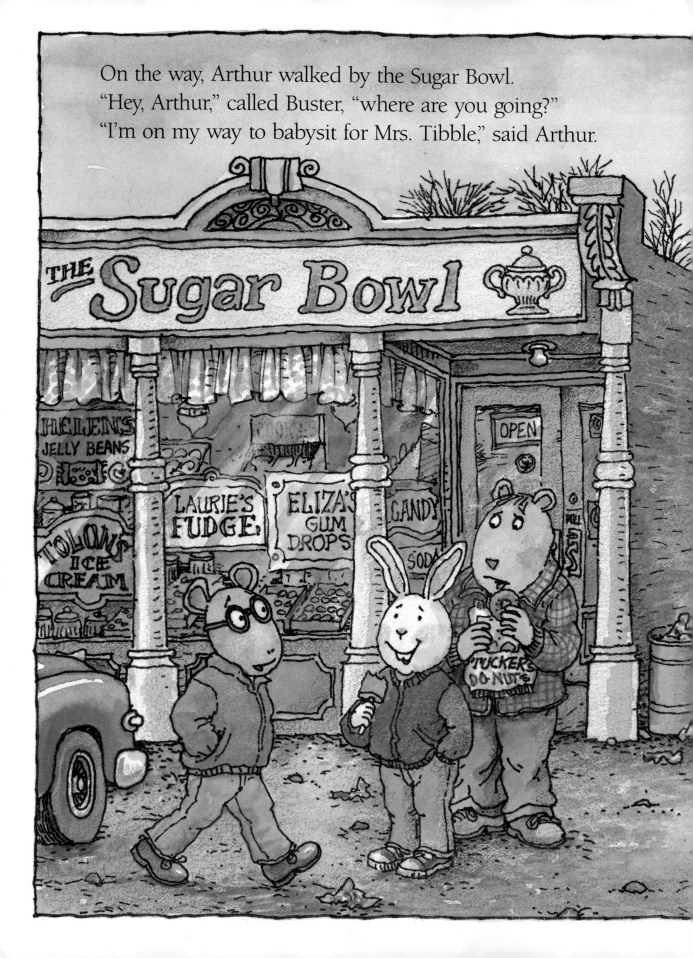

"Not the terrible Tibble twins!" gasped Prunella. "My sister babysat for them once. And once was enough."

"You can always back out," said Buster, ". . . while you're still alive."

"Don't worry," said Francine. "It will be just like babysitting D.W. and baby Kate."

Arthur remembered what that was like!

Now he was really worried.

Mrs. Tibble was waiting for Arthur.

"I'm so glad you're here," she said. "And so are the twins. This is little Tommy in red, and Timmy's in blue. Almost bedtime, darlings! I'll be back soon."

"Very soon, I hope," said Arthur.

"Nighty-night, Grammy," said the twins sweetly.

"She's gone!" screamed the twins. "Playtime!"

"No, *bed*time," said Arthur.
"We're not sleepy," said Timmy.

The phone rang. It was D.W.

"I called with some advice," she said. "Calm them down with a quiet game . . . like cards."

"Thanks," said Arthur. "Bye."

"How about a nice quiet game of cards?" asked Arthur.

"Great!" said the twins.

"We know a really good card game. . . ." said Tommy.

"Fifty-two pick-up!" they screamed.
Just then the phone rang again. It was D.W.
"Sounds like they're out of control," she said. "You need to show them who's boss!"
"Thanks a lot," said Arthur.

"Let's play cowboys!" said Tommy.
"I'll be the sheriff," said Arthur, "because I'm the boss."
"And we'll be the bad guys," said Timmy.

The next time the phone rang, Timmy answered it.
"Arthur can't come to the phone right now," he said.
"He's all tied up."
"Time for hide-and-seek!" called Tommy. "You'll never
find us!"

When Arthur finally got loose, he searched and searched.
If I don't find them soon, he thought, I'll be in big trouble.

Just then the phone rang again.

"What's going on over there?" asked D.W. "Shouldn't they be in bed?"

"I can't talk now," said Arthur. "I'm looking for the twins."

"You mean you lost them?" shouted D.W.

"Not exactly," he said. "I just can't find them."

"You're in really big trouble!" said D.W. "What are you going to do?"

Just then Arthur noticed the curtains wiggling.
"You'll see," he said. "I sure hope I find them before the
swamp thing does!" he added loudly.
"Swamp thing?" asked Tommy from behind the curtain.

"Yes, the one that comes out on nights just like tonight,"
Arthur said. "Sit down and I'll tell you about it."
Arthur used his spookiest voice. "Once in a dark, spooky
swamp, there lived a horrible, big, slimy, stinky green
swamp thing," he began.
"You mean like a monster?" Tommy asked meekly.
"Exactly," said Arthur, "with long, sharp teeth. And the
swamp thing realized it was very, very hungry," said Arthur.
"It left the swamp in search of dinner."
"What did it like to eat?" Timmy asked in a shaky voice.
"Boys," said Arthur. "Especially twin boys."

The twins moved closer to Arthur.

"The swamp thing began to moan from hunger," continued Arthur, "until it came to a big old house, just like this one."

"I hear footsteps!" cried Timmy.

"It's only your imagination," said Arthur. "Want to sit on my lap?"

"Well, just for a minute," said Timmy.

"Slowly . . ." whispered Arthur, "with its big slimy green hand, the swamp thing opened the front door. . . . 'I smell dinner,' it said. It licked its lips."

"Help!" screamed the twins.

"It's coming in *our* front door!" yelled Timmy.

Just then the door *did* open, and the lights went on.

"I'm home!" said Mrs. Tibble. "And look at my little angels. Arthur must be a wonderful babysitter."

"He's not scared of anything," said Timmy.

"And he tells great stories, too!" said Tommy. "We want him to babysit again."

The twins hugged Arthur good night.

Then Mrs. Tibble paid Arthur and thanked him for doing such a fine job.

When Arthur got home, D.W. was still up.
"You're home early," she said. "Did you get fired?"
"No," said Arthur. "Babysitting isn't so bad. Mrs Tibble thinks I'm pretty good at it. Now she wants me to babysit the twins every afternoon right here at our house. And . . .